THE FRONT ROOM

MICHELLE MAGORIAN

With illustrations by
Vladimir Stankovic

Barrington Stoke

For Lexie Hamblin, with thanks

First published in 2016 in Great Britain by
Barrington Stoke Ltd
18 Walker Street, Edinburgh, EH3 7LP

www.barringtonstoke.co.uk

Text © 2016 Michelle Magorian
Illustrations © 2016 Vladimir Stankovic

A CIP catalogue record for this book is available
from the British Library upon request

ISBN: 978-1-78112-501-4

Printed in China by Leo

CONTENTS

CHAPTER ONE

Luck

Hannah woke up with a start. Her face was to the wall, and she felt again that awful presence behind her. She took a deep breath, gritted her teeth, and forced herself to look round. In the half-dark, shadows moved. She pushed herself out of bed, sprinted across the room and turned on the light.

All Hannah could see was her bed up by the window, a faded sofa, two armchairs, a shabby carpet, and a table and two chairs up against the wall by the door. Even so, she decided to keep the light on. Her parents would be furious if she woke them up for the fourth night in a row. When she had dashed into their room the night before, their patience had snapped.

"There's nothing wrong with that room," her mum had said. "You're acting like a baby. Anybody would think you were two years old – not fourteen."

"You know your mother needs a good rest," her dad said. "If I have any more of this nonsense, I'll stop your pocket money."

Hannah was desperate for that pocket money. For over a year she had been practising on a friend's guitar while she saved up for her own. Her parents had even promised that if she helped out and did some baby-sitting they'd pay her the same as a proper baby-sitter. But she was also desperate not to sleep in the front room.

"Couldn't I sleep with Benjy?" she asked.

Benjy was Hannah's brother. He was three. He slept at the end of the corridor in a small room which led into the kitchen.

"Don't be silly, Hannah," her mum snapped. "It's only a little sofa bed."

"But, Mum –" Hannah had protested.

"That is *enough*," her dad said. "Now cut it out."

Hannah had given up and skulked back to her room. She clambered into bed with a sigh. Ever since Mum had lost the baby, her parents always seemed to be snapping at Hannah and Benjy, and at each other too.

Hannah pulled the curtains aside and stared out at the dark street below. Dad kept saying how lucky they'd been to find this holiday flat at all, and how the old woman who owned the place had gone out of her way to put a bed in the front room for Hannah. But it didn't feel very lucky to her.

CHAPTER TWO

Kiddo

As soon as it was dawn Hannah felt it was safe enough to go back to sleep. She'd only just closed her eyes when an angry voice woke her up again.

"Did you sleep with the light on all night?"

"No, Dad," Hannah said. "Only a bit of it. I didn't want to wake you up again."

Her dad sat on the bed. He was a big man with a round nose and untidy brown hair. Hannah was small, but apart from that she was the spitting image of him.

"Look, kiddo." He always called her that when he treated her special. "What's up?"

Hannah pushed herself up onto her elbows. "I don't know," she said. "One minute I'm asleep and then I wake up and I can feel someone in the room."

Her father looked awkward. "Look," he said. "I know me and your mum haven't been getting on too well the last few weeks. We're both tired and we're both a bit upset because of the baby. You know."

"Yeah," Hannah said.

"It's just a bad patch, that's all," her dad said. "It's hard for your mum, but she's already looking a bit perkier. The sea air's cheering her up. I know it's not much of a holiday for you, but if you could just keep on helping to look after Benjy, it'd make a lot of difference."

Hannah sat up, puzzled. "But you know I'm happy to do that, Dad," she said.

And it was true. She liked looking after Benjy, so that her parents could have some time together. It made her feel useful, important.

"I thought maybe you were a bit fed up of him and were trying to get your own back," her father said.

"Dad!"

"I just wanted to make sure," he said, and he stood up. "I'll get breakfast going, eh? My bacon and scrambled egg special today for you, kiddo." And he gave a broad grin.

Hannah grinned back and pushed the duvet aside.

CHAPTER THREE

Tingle

Hannah's first job in the morning was to wash and dress Benjy. Mum had her breakfast in bed on a tray. Dad wouldn't let her get up for breakfast all holiday. That morning, Hannah and Benjy stuck a little bunch of flowers in an empty jam jar filled with water, and her dad placed it on the tray and carried it in to her mum. He ate a big pile of bacon and egg with them and then he took another mug of tea into the bedroom, while Hannah washed up.

Benjy stood on the chair by the sink and pretended to be useful, but really he just made a lot of mess on the floor. Hannah put her arm around him and pressed her cheek against his.

"Want some milk," he demanded.

"OK," she said. "But first you can help me make the sandwiches."

Hannah was peeling off squares of cheese from a packet for Benjy to put on the bread when she heard her parents walk through the little room where Benjy slept. As soon as her mum opened the door, Hannah looked up at her.

To Hannah's relief she saw that the grey shadows under her mum's eyes had at last begun to disappear. She even had some colour in her cheeks. She was wearing her sea-green dressing gown, with her long black hair scooped back from her face.

"Clever boy, Benjy. You're making some lovely sandwiches there," she said with a smile. "But you're looking very peaky, Hannah. You didn't have another bad dream, did you?" she asked.

"Too much reading," Dad jumped in.

"Yeah," Hannah said. "I got this amazing book. I couldn't put it down last night."

Hannah finished making the sandwiches and then she began to collect towels and buckets. Benjy trailed after her as she walked through his room, down the long narrow corridor and up to the door of the front room. She pushed it open. Her bag was hanging from the back of a chair over by the table.

"Want some milk," Benjy said again.

"In a minute."

Benjy scowled and sat down in the corner, where he began to trace the patterns on the faded carpet with his fingers.

Hannah picked up a towel and swimsuit and shoved them into the bag. She slung it over her arm and then leaned out of the window. The sea was only five minutes' walk away.

As Hannah gazed out at the blue line of the sea, she felt a cold tingle move down the back of her neck, right to the base of her spine. It was as though someone was touching her with ice-cold fingers. She whirled around but she could see nothing, only Benjy sitting on the carpet. It was as if whatever it was slipped behind her back every time she moved. She pressed herself against the wall. Without thinking, her hand went up to her throat as if to protect it. She shivered and pushed herself away.

"Come on, Benjy," she said, and she hauled

him up from the floor.

She wanted to run out the room with him, but instead she forced herself to walk slowly, so as not to alarm him.

CHAPTER FOUR

Monotony

That night they had dinner in a pub down by the harbour, where they could sit and look out at all the boats coming in to moor. It wasn't until they had eaten that Hannah raised the subject of the front room. As soon as Hannah's mum took Benjy to the loo, she grabbed her chance.

"Dad," she said, "could we change where my bed is and put it by the opposite wall?"

"Oh, Hannah," he warned. "Don't you start on about that room again."

"I'm not starting," Hannah said. "I just want the bed moved, that's all. I think it's the rattling of the windows that's scaring me."

Her dad smiled. "Piece of cake, kiddo. We'll shift it as soon as we get back."

Hannah could have wept with relief. At least she'd feel a bit safer up by the wall of her parents' bedroom and she'd be nearer the light switch.

As soon as they got back from the pub, Hannah and her dad moved the bed. Her mum was happy about it too.

"I thought she was catching a bit of a chill by that window," her mum said. Hannah's dad just winked at Hannah.

After Benjy had gone to bed, Hannah and her parents played Monopoly. She didn't care for the game much. It was too slow and seemed to go on for hours. "Monotony," she called it. But it was different that night. Her mum was smiling and joking. So was her dad. When it was time for Hannah to go to bed, the last sound she heard was her parents chatting over a game of cards.

CHAPTER FIVE

Breath

At first Hannah thought it was the sound of her own breathing that had woken her, but she realised with a start that the breathing was coming from someone else. It was a rasping, wheezy sort of breath. She sat up and peered into the darkness.

A floorboard creaked. The sound came from the direction of the window. It was followed a half-second later by another creak.

There was no mistaking it – someone was in the room. Hannah listened, terrified, as the creaking grew louder and nearer, and the breathing turned into great heaving gasps.

Hannah jumped out of bed, turned on the light and looked around the room in terror. There was no one there. She was shaking with fear as she backed out of the door. She would spend the rest of the night in the kitchen.

CHAPTER SIX

Nightmare

Hannah sat at the kitchen table and waited. The dawn was a long time coming. Even when it started to grow light outside, she had no idea of the time. She pressed her ear up against the radio, with the volume on low. Anything to hear the comforting sounds of a voice and early morning pop music.

At eight o'clock, Hannah turned the sound up and began to lay the table. She was just pouring milk into a jug, when the door knob moved. She jumped. Benjy opened the door, his eyes sticky with sleep.

"Oh, Benjy," Hannah said. She picked him up and gave him a squeeze. "I'm so glad to see you."

"Want some milk," Benjy said, and he rubbed his eyes.

As Hannah sat Benjy down, her parents walked in, still in their pyjamas.

"Hello, Dad," Hannah said with a bright smile, to hide her tiredness. "Thought I'd make us all a surprise breakfast. I'll put the kettle on."

Her dad eyed her suspiciously. "I didn't hear you get up."

"Hannah, go back to bed," her mum said. "You look awful."

"I'm all right."

"Course she is," her dad said. "Come on, let's get the breakfast started."

Hannah knew she had to get her dad on his own, but it wasn't until the afternoon that her chance came. They were rushing back to the holiday flat after lunch in a café on the seafront. It was raining and her mum had run on ahead, pushing Benjy in his buggy.

Hannah grabbed her dad by the arm. "Dad, I've got to tell you about last night!"

"I know about last night," he said. "You had another of your nightmares, I suppose."

They had stopped in a doorway to watch the wind whipping rain along the harbour wall. People in flimsy summer clothes ran for shelter. Some had plastic bags held above their heads.

"Please, listen to me, Dad," Hannah said. "I heard footsteps and this horrible breathing."

He turned to look at her. "What?" he said. His voice was sharp.

"Honest, Dad," Hannah said. "It was over by the window. I thought it was a nightmare but I sat right up in bed and the sounds got louder and started to come towards me."

Her dad started to walk on. Hannah had to run to keep up with him. "But when I turned the light on," she went on, "there was no one there."

"Well, there you are then," he said. "It must have been a bad dream."

Hannah glared at him. "But why would I have all these bad dreams all of a sudden? Why now? Please, Dad, you have to believe me." Hannah shoved her hands in the pockets of her jeans.

"Look, kiddo," her dad began.

"Don't call me kiddo!" Hannah snapped.

"Well, you're acting like a kid!" he said. There was real anger in his voice now. "Are you trying to scare everyone with these stupid nightmares?"

"They're *not* nightmares!" Hannah yelled. "I've told you – I'm awake when it happens."

Hannah stormed on ahead, swallowing her tears and rage while the rain lashed across her face. One minute adults expected you to be grown up, but if you tried to talk to them they refused to listen. If a grown-up had told her dad the story of the front room, he'd have listened all right.

At last Hannah stopped, scared and miserable. Her dad ran up next to her and pulled her under his umbrella. He drew her close to him and gave her a big hug. Before she could stop herself, Hannah burst into tears. She understood for a moment how her mum must have been feeling. She was so tired. She'd give anything for a good night's sleep.

"Look," her dad said, and his voice was calm and quiet, "we've only got a few days left."

"I know, Dad, but I can't sleep in that front room again, I just can't."

He took out a hankie and wiped her face. "Don't worry, kiddo, we'll sort something out."

CHAPTER SEVEN

Pencil

Later, in the kitchen, Hannah's dad took her to one side. Benjy was asleep in his little bed and her mum had gone into the bedroom to get changed.

"Are you sure you'll be all right on your own?" her dad asked.

Hannah nodded.

"We'll be at the pub down by the harbour," he said. "The one we went to the other day. We'll only be gone an hour. Call us on your mobile if you're worried about anything."

"I'll be fine, Dad," Hannah said. "Stay longer if you want. I'll sit here in the kitchen."

"No, we'll come straight back," he said. "You look like you could do with an early night." He paused. "I still don't know where we're going to put you."

"I'll make up a bed in the bath," Hannah said, grinning.

Dad ruffled her hair. "Atta girl."

Hannah kissed her mum goodbye and told them a million times she'd be fine. Then, after her parents had left, she settled down at the kitchen table to read her book. It

wasn't until later that she had to go into the front room. She'd started to scribble down some verses for a song and had run out of paper. She knew that there was an exercise book on the table in her room.

"Oh, come on," she whispered to herself. "It's only a stupid room, and it isn't even dark yet."

As soon as she stepped into the room she sensed that the evil that had been there had disappeared. It was as if it had been somehow swept away by a powerful force. Hannah didn't feel scared any more. She shut the door behind her, picked up the exercise book and sat down on the bed. She had thought of a word for her song to rhyme with "panes" and wanted to write it down in case she forgot it. "Lanes," she scribbled.

It was so cosy and comfortable in the room that Hannah stayed there, as the words to her song flowed smoothly.

Rain like silver water.

Rattling the panes.

Shaking all the branches.

Muddying the lanes.

Sailors in their oilskins.

Rain slips down their necks.

She paused to rack her brain for a word
to rhyme with "necks", and her eyelids began
to flicker. Within minutes, her head sank
back onto the pillow and the pencil slipped
from her fingers.

CHAPTER EIGHT

Mirror

Hannah had no idea what time it was when she woke up. She only knew that it felt like the middle of the night. Light from the street lamp outside spilled across the carpet in eerie patterns. She struggled to shake off her fear, but it was no good. She knew that something had woken her, and that it was still somewhere in the room. She turned her head and saw the tiled fireplace, the corner where an old CD player stood near a handful of books on a shelf, the window with its fluttering curtains, and the

wall stretching along to the table.

And then she saw him. A tall man,
standing in the shadows. He had dark,
straggly hair and a black beard. His arms
hung by his sides, still.

Hannah turned her head away.

'It's a nightmare,' she told herself. 'I'm dreaming that I've woken up.'

She squeezed her eyes shut, trying to convince herself that it was a dream. But then there was a slight breath of air by the bed. Hannah opened her eyes. The man was now towering above her.

'I'm dreaming this,' she told herself. 'I'm dreaming, I'm dreaming, I'm dreaming.'

The man leaned towards her.

Please let me wake up soon.

But the dark shadow loomed nearer and she felt strong hands grip her round the throat.

With one enormous effort Hannah struggled free and scrambled backwards. She half stumbled, half fell over the back of the bed. In utter terror, she switched the light on. The room was empty.

Hannah flung the door open and ran through Benjy's room into the kitchen. Once she was in there, she felt safe. She slid the window up and leaned out, gasping. She shivered and looked around for her hoodie. It was then that she caught sight of herself in the small cracked mirror above the sink. She gave a startled cry, for there on her neck were the red marks made by the man's hands. She hadn't imagined him, after all.

Hannah opened the door into her brother's room, ran in and dragged him out of bed.

CHAPTER NINE

Shelter

Hannah stood outside the pub by the harbour. Rain was lashing her face, and her arms were sore from the effort of carrying Benjy. She unzipped her wet jacket and wrapped it round him in an effort to keep him dry. Then she found a door and slipped inside.

The man behind the bar spotted her at once. "'Ere," he said. "Outside!"

"I'm looking for my mum and dad,"
Hannah said. "Please. It's important."

"Phone them then," the barman said.

"I've left my mobile in the holiday flat."

Hannah felt her face grow red as
everyone turned to look at her.

"Go back and call them from there then,"
the barman said.

"But I can't –" she began.

"Out!" said the man. "No kids in here at
night – it's the rules."

Outside, the sea was hurling itself against the harbour wall. Hannah could hardly see for the spray in her eyes. There was another pub a small way off. Hannah lowered her head and hugged Benjy to her as she pushed against the swirl of wind.

After half an hour of looking through pub
windows, she still hadn't found Mum and
Dad. She stumbled back along the beach
and into a shelter where there were some
wooden seats. Hannah was exhausted. Benjy
was shivering and had begun to sob with the
cold. She started to rub his hands. She was

in the middle of singing him her new song to try to calm him down, when she heard heavy footsteps approach the shelter. She froze for an instant, and then she bundled Benjy up again, shot out of the shelter and ran.

The footsteps got faster. Suddenly someone gripped Hannah from behind and twisted her round. She opened her mouth to scream – only to find that she was peering up at two policemen.

They didn't listen to her either. All they said was something about getting dry and looking after the little chap and finding her parents. Even when she and Benjy were sitting in the warm police station, with mugs of tea and milk in their hands, the policeman who'd stayed with her just kept shaking his head and muttering, "Kids!"

It was only when Hannah gave him the address of the holiday home that he began to look interested.

"It's five minutes from the sea," she said. "In St Andrew's Road."

The sergeant had been standing with her back to them, but she swung round, startled. "St Andrew's?" she said. "A top floor flat?"

Hannah nodded.

"And you say that you think a man was trying to kill you?"

"Yes." Hannah began to shiver. "I felt his hands around my neck, but when I turned on the light he wasn't there."

"It wouldn't be number 43, would it?" the sergeant asked. Her voice was gentle now.

"Yes, that's right."

"Woodfield," the sergeant said to the young constable, "see if a Mr and Mrs Robinson are in the top flat at number 43."

"But they might not be there," Hannah blurted out. "I don't know where they are, but if they aren't there ... I'm not going back there on my own."

"Don't worry, lass," the policeman said. "You won't have to."

Hannah leaned back in relief and sipped her tea. Benjy was curled up on the bench beside her with his head on her leg, fast asleep.

By the time Hannah had finished her third cup of tea, the two police officers returned with her parents. Her mum was in a terrible state – her face was grey and streaked with

tears. Her dad, on the other hand, was

furious.

"Where the hell have you been?" he yelled. He looked like he was about to explode. "Me and your mum have been worried sick."

"Mr Robinson," the sergeant said. "I'd like to speak to you and your wife in private."

"We only left them for an hour –" her dad began.

"Please," said the sergeant.

Hannah watched as they went into the room next door. She did her best to listen from the bench but the two police officers looking after her cottoned on, and they started to ask her boring questions about school.

When Hannah's parents reappeared, they looked stunned. Her father gave her a strange look.

"What's the matter, Dad?" Hannah asked.

"Come on," he said. "We're going to move into a B&B."

From then on, it was all a blur. All Hannah could remember was a trip up a wide staircase with a striped carpet, then a soak in a warm bath, before her mum wrapped her up in a big soft towel.

CHAPTER TEN

A Different Tune

When Hannah woke up the next morning, she found that she was lying in a comfy bed with a pile of grey-blue pillows on it. Her mother was sitting at a table, writing postcards.

"What time is it?" Hannah asked.

Her mother turned and smiled. "Eleven o'clock," she said. "You've been asleep for twelve hours."

She came and sat on the bed and smoothed Hannah's fringe behind her ears. "Hurry up and get dressed," she said. "Your dad's taken Benjy to the beach, but you and me, we'll go down to that fisherman's caff by the harbour and have a big fry-up."

At the café Hannah tucked into egg, bacon, fried bread, tomatoes, sausages and two large mugs of tea. Only then would her mum at last answer her questions about the holiday flat.

"Are you sure you want to know?" she asked.

"Oh, Mum!" said Hannah. "Course I do."

"Well," her mum began, "nearly sixty years ago, a man murdered three children in that front room."

Hannah felt sick. "That's terrible!" she whispered.

Her mum leaned over and touched Hannah's arm. "Poor little things. They were all girls."

Hannah's fingers moved up towards her neck as if to protect it. "He strangled them, didn't he?" she said.

Her mum nodded and looked out the window.

"They must have been so scared," Hannah said, and all of a sudden she felt overwhelmed with sadness for them. "But this man can't still be alive, can he?" she added in alarm.

"Of course not, love," her mum said. "He was hanged. That's what they did to murderers back then."

"But I felt his hands." Hannah looked hard at her mother. "Honest, Mum, I really did. He made red marks on my neck."

"Look, love, I believe you," Mum said. She took hold of Hannah's hands and squeezed them. "I wish I'd known. I'd never have let you sleep in there." She gave a shudder. "But it's all over now. We'll have a lovely day together and stay at that nice B&B from now on."

Hannah sighed with relief and gazed at the heavy drizzle which had begun to fall outside. It didn't look much like a lovely day ...

Just then she felt a heavy hand on her shoulder. She gave a startled yell and whirled around in her chair.

"Dad!" she cried, as Benjy flung his arms around her. "Don't do that! You scared me half to death!"

"Sorry," he said.

Hannah noticed that there was a sheepish grin on his face and that he was holding both his hands behind his back.

"Dad!" Hannah said. "What are you hiding?"

He placed a large wooden object in her lap.

"Oh, Dad!" she exclaimed. "A guitar!"

It was a Spanish one. Just like a real folk singer's. Hannah let her hands glide over its polished wooden curves.

"I spotted it in the window of a second-hand shop round the corner," her dad said. "It's got nice new strings, but might have got a bit damp from the rain." He took out his hankie and wiped a few drops from the guitar.

"Oh, Dad," Hannah whispered, and beamed at him. "Thank you."

Within minutes, her head was bowed over the guitar and her thumb and fingers were plucking the strings. Contented, she hummed along to the tune of her new song.

"Rain like silver water," she sang in a soft voice. *"Rattling the panes. Shaking all the branches. Muddying the lanes."*

Little by little her parents' voices faded into the distance. She didn't even hear her brother asking for more milk.

"*Rain falls on the sailors, sliding down their necks, running down the wooden masts, bouncing off the decks.*"

Hannah was at one with her guitar, lost in the sound its strings made against the wood. Maybe she could write a song for the three little girls, one that would make them feel happy and not scared any more. And then she remembered the baby her mum had lost. She would write a song for him, too. A special one.

Hannah smiled. Lost in her music, she had quite forgotten that she was sitting in a fisherman's caff down by the harbour. And the murderer's ghost? She had forgotten him, too.

Our books are tested
for children and young people by
children and young people.

Thanks to everyone who consulted on
a manuscript for their time and effort in
helping us to make our books better
for our readers.